Detour on Halloween Night

NEAL LOVETT

authorHOUSE®

AuthorHouse™
1663 Liberty Drive
Bloomington, IN 47403
www.authorhouse.com
Phone: 1 (800) 839-8640

Published by AuthorHouse 01/07/2019

ISBN: 978-1-5462-6905-2 (sc)

Print information available on the last page.

This book is printed on acid-free paper.

For a daughter of the prairie

1

Taylor tied Betsy, his old mare, to the hitching post and entered the tavern. "What brings you in so late, Mr. Taylor?" the barman asked. "It's well past dark."

"I finished a trial and got a late start home," Taylor said. "I'll say the woods are beautiful."

"The leaves are turning. It's a lovely time of year," the barman said. "And you surely know what tonight is?"

"Wednesday."

"And?"

"It's All Hallows' Eve, isn't it?" Taylor said.

"Yes, it is." The barman set a beer down for Taylor. "So you'd better fortify yourself against the chill. Now that we enter the dark season, it's easier for them to enter our world. There will be bonfires tonight. It's said the fire protects us, helps to keep them from entering our world."

"I won't speak of them," Taylor said.

"It's just as well," the barman said.

"The Scots and Irish have surely brought this night to our country, haven't they?"

The barman nodded, then served a plate of food to one of the few customers who sat scattered in the dimly lit tavern.

"You're a MacFall, aren't you?" Taylor asked the barman.

"Aye, that I am," the barman answered. "And I dare say they're not celebrating this night in New England."

"I think not."

"They're surely different from us Virginians, aren't they?" mused the barman.

"It's been that way from the beginning of the colonies," Taylor said. "Even back in England we were different. During the English Civil War, Virginians returned to fight for the king, but New Englanders went back to fight for Cromwell."

"I did not know that," MacFall said. "Where did your ancestors come from?"

"My first ancestor was from Lancashire," Taylor said. "He was bound."

"An indentured servant?"

"Indeed. He was a farm laborer. It wasn't the nicest life, I'm sure. Stories have come down through the family."

"I, too, have ancestors who were bound," MacFall said.

"Then you know."

"By the way," MacFall said, "what do you think of the law passed in Washington last year, the one meant to solve the slavery question?"

"The Missouri Compromise?"

The barman nodded. "That's it."

"It will take time to know."

"Mr. Taylor, my wife and I would like to have a will prepared, especially now that we own the tavern."

"That's a good idea. There comes a time when we must leave this earth and part with our loved ones."

"And there comes a time when we're forced to be generous," MacFall said, smiling, "in anticipation of death."

Taylor laughed. "Come now, MacFall. You're a generous man."

"And because you're an intelligent man––"

"Then why can't I spell *Cincinnati?*" Taylor interrupted.

Now MacFall laughed. "Well, we'd like you to write our will, anyway."

They talked a while longer before Taylor laid some coins on the bar and donned his coat and hat.

"Good night, Mr. Taylor. And do guard your privy. The lads will be out tonight."

"And tipping over outhouses," Taylor said. "Yes, I know. I may have done it myself as a lad. Thank you, MacFall. Good night."

Taylor stepped into the chilly darkness and untied Betsy. Betsy began a modest trot, *clip-clop, clip-clop,* before Taylor slowed her. The sound of Betsy's hooves meeting the dirt road rose above the buzz of insects, faint now in autumn's chill, and the occasional rush of wind in the trees. Every critter's scamper or rustle of leaves was a source of mystery in the darkness, for darkness changes everything. And it was still a dark world, a world lit by fire.

An owl hooted. Taylor jumped in his saddle. After a while he saw light back in the woods. Beyond a bend in the road, the light became clearer, and he smelled smoke. He could see the fire now, back in a clearing. Surely it was a bonfire of which MacFall spoke. As the road took him closer, he could see the fire's size and hear the crackle and pop of burning wood. There was singing, and people moved around the fire.

Taylor passed the fire, and the light faded. Soon he rode again in darkness. Before long, he was out of the deeper woods and passed farmhouses with dimly lit windows. He was only a few miles from home.

Suddenly Betsy reared up. "Whoa, Betsy, whoa," he pleaded, pulling on the reins. "It's all right."

Then he heard sounds, which grew louder as he rode. There was a humming noise, which rose and then faded. As he rode on, he heard more distinctly the sound build, peak, then fade away. And there was light. At first it was dim and distant. As the light moved, it became brighter and clearer. Like the sound, the light peaked and then faded. Taylor wondered if the light was moving fire, except that the light was white. And how could fire move that fast?

Taylor rode on toward home, and the light and sound grew more intense. Some sounds were louder than others, and some were really loud. Now he could make out multiple lights, two and three at a time, seeming to move in many directions through the woods, building, peaking, then receding. His ride had been peaceful. Now this.

Soon the noise became extremely loud, unlike anything he had ever heard. He covered his ears with his hands. As Betsy brought him closer to the disturbance, he could see bright centers of light, from which greater light spread out.

Betsy was spooked. She would go no farther. Taylor dismounted, tied her to a tree, and walked closer to the noise and light. He was now about thirty yards away, and he could clearly see that the centers of light were attached to objects, and the objects were moving both directions. There were also red lights on the ends of the objects and also on top of the larger ones. They moved at incredible speed, faster than the fastest horse, perhaps even faster than birds diving in the sky.

Taylor walked closer and climbed an embankment to stand close to a hard surface. He was now near the moving objects. The objects nearest him moved one direction, to his right, and the others, across the way, moved the opposite direction.

The noise was deafening. The biggest objects made the most noise. They were long and boxlike, with red lights all over, and sometimes blew him back when they passed.

"I cannot believe this," he said softly. He thought how his wife sometimes told him he was not alert to the peril of life. Taylor was no longer a young man, nor did he yet understand life's sad reality.

He thought he saw faces of people in the passing objects, behind windows, but he wasn't sure. He knew stagecoaches and roads and thought this could be something similar, yet entirely different. He stamped his foot on the ground, then on the hard surface, to prove he was on *terra firma* and not in a dream. His boot met resistance.

Fear surged through him. He ran down the embankment toward the road on which he'd been traveling, where he'd tied Betsy to a tree. He walked for some time but couldn't find the road. There was only an empty field and darkness, and no sign of Betsy.

Taylor went back up the embankment and stood again next to the hard surface. The objects still sped by, and he was blown back again by the large objects as they passed. Now he was certain he saw faces in the passing objects. Some of the faces even turned toward him. These were faces of people, faces of human beings like him and MacFall and the people in his town. He also saw people, usually one man, sitting high up in the front of the big, long objects.

After a while, Taylor descended the embankment once more but again could find neither the road nor Betsy. So he returned to his place near the hard surface. Though fearful, he was also curious about this incredible occurrence that was happening to him. He wondered if he was in a different place, something very unlike what he had known all his life.

He'd stood there for a few minutes when one of the objects slowed as it passed him, its rear red lights brightening.

The object came to a complete stop, and the red lights now dimmed, just off the hard surface about seventy-five yards beyond Taylor. Then the object, its rear white lights brightening, slowly moved backward and stopped about ten yards from him. The object was bigger than most of the others that passed on the hard surface but smaller than the largest ones.

Taylor was sweating now. Was he in danger? Should he run? Then what appeared to be a door on the object opened, and a man stepped out and walked toward him. A beam of light seemed to project from the man's hand. Taylor's heart beat wildly, but he held his ground. The man stopped just in front of him. The man was five or six inches taller than Taylor and wore a hat with a bill in front.

"Mister, are you all right?" the man asked, almost shouting to be heard above the deafening noise.

"Yes," Taylor said, shading the truth.

"Do you need a ride?" Taylor didn't know what to say. "Are you homeless?" the man asked, still speaking loudly.

"Please?"

"Do you have a place to sleep tonight?" the man asked, then waved his arm to move Taylor farther from the speeding vehicles. "You're too close to the road. It's dangerous."

Taylor stepped back from the edge of the road.

"You live around here?" the man asked.

"Indeed," Taylor answered, "we live just outside town."

"Are you hitchhiking?"

7

"Hitch ...?"

"Are you trying to get a ride?"

"No."

"It's dangerous to be walking on the highway," the man said. "And it might be illegal."

"Illegal?" Taylor asked. It was a word that got his attention.

"Yes. It might be against the law," the man said.

"I understand."

The man waited for vehicles to pass, then asked with a lowered voice, which sounded flat to Taylor, "Why don't you get in our motorhome? It's safe, and you can decide what you want to do. We'll drive you home if you want."

"Yes, I'll do that," Taylor said, judging the man to be safe. The man led Taylor to the vehicle with his light. The man opened its door and directed Taylor to a seat just behind the two front seats. A woman sat in the front passenger seat, and a young man, drinking from a small can, sat behind Taylor.

Taylor noticed the pretty orange light coming from directly in front of the seated man. The man had called the vehicle a motorhome, and it appeared to be a sort of home. It was outfitted with chairs, beds, and a table with seats, and there appeared to be a sort of kitchen.

Taylor sat quietly as the couple communicated discreetly. They moved their lips without speaking and read each other's eyes. Taylor read the woman's lips when she silently asked,

"Are you sure he's safe?" The man's answer was a tiny shrug. He wasn't sure. There was tension now.

The man turned to Taylor and said, "We're traveling to the Midwest toward Chicago. We'll give you a few minutes to decide what you want to do."

"I wonder if I *can* go home," Taylor blurted, in a spasm of honesty.

"Marital problems?" the man asked.

"No."

"If you don't have a place to go," the man said, "we can take you to a motel, or a shelter. Or you can continue on with us."

Taylor thought hard, trying to focus, pushing his mind to make sense of his situation and decide what to do. So much had happened so quickly. The man was offering to take him home, back to Ann and the children, but he'd tried to find the road and Betsy twice, without success. He now seemed sure that something had truly changed, that he'd been pulled into something and some *place* he didn't understand, which was beyond his control.

Now Taylor had to decide. It was a big decision, and he knew it. These people were taking a chance on him. Somehow he trusted them. Maybe it was their sweet faces. They seemed to be kind, but they surely smiled a lot. And their teeth were so white. He had never seen such big, healthy-looking teeth.

He figured that if he didn't continue on with these people in their motorhome, he would be back on the four-lane highway. And what then?

"I'll go with you," Taylor said.

"Fine," the man said. He carefully guided the vehicle back onto the highway. "It's Saturday night and getting late, so there shouldn't be much traffic. We should make good time."

"You say it's Saturday night?" Taylor asked.

"Yes."

"Isn't it Wednesday?"

"No."

"Is it All Hallows' Eve?" Taylor asked.

"It's Halloween, if that's what you mean," the man answered. "By the way, I'm Bob Larkin, and this is my wife, Cathy. And that's Chris behind you, drinking the soda pop."

"My name is Taylor."

"Is that your Halloween costume?" Cathy asked. "You're a colonial?"

"To help you get a ride?" Bob said.

"This is not a costume," Taylor answered firmly. "These are my clothes. I am not a colonial. Virginia is no longer a colony, nor is Maryland or North Carolina. The states are free now, free of British rule. We are the United States of America."

"Of course," Bob said.

"And we've added states to the Union since the Revolution," Taylor said.

"Would you like a cup of coffee, Mr. Taylor?" Cathy asked. "Or a soda pop?"

"A pop?"

"Yes, a soda pop," Cathy said, pointing at Chris's can.

"I'll have coffee, thank you."

"We're coming from the DC area," Bob said. "We picked up Chris at his college."

"You live in Washington?" Taylor asked.

"We live near there," Cathy said. "The younger kids are unhappy about missing trick-or-treating, but they got to do some before we left home."

"We tried to explain to the kids that there will be more Halloweens," Bob said, "but I don't think they're too happy."

"We love Halloween," Cathy said. "My family has been celebrating Halloween for generations."

"Where did you say you are traveling?" Taylor asked.

"To Chicago," Bob answered.

"Where is this located?"

"You've never heard of Chicago?" Cathy asked.

"No, ma'am."

"Chicago, Illinois?" Cathy said.

"I've heard of Illinois," Taylor said. "Illinois entered the Union not long ago, and I believe there is an Illinois River."

"Chicago's on Lake Michigan," Bob said. "Do you know Lake Michigan?"

"It's one of the big lakes out west," Taylor said. "How many people live in Chicago?"

"There's about eight million in Chicagoland," Bob said.

"I see," Taylor said and considered that the 1820 census had counted fewer than a million Virginians and ten million Americans.

"Winters are cold in Chicago," Cathy said.

"Colder than here?" Taylor asked.

The Larkins smiled and then chimed, "Yes."

"And the summers are hot," Bob added. "But they're great for baseball. You know baseball?"

"Baseball?" Taylor said.

"Yeah," Bob said. "A guy throws a ball, a really hard ball, and another guy tries to hit the ball with a wooden bat."

"That sounds like rounders," Taylor said.

"Yes, like rounders," Bob said.

"I've played rounders," Taylor said.

"You've play rounders?" Bob asked. "The game from the 1800s."

"Yes."

Cathy looked at her husband with her bright blue eyes stretched wide.

"Is it some sort of commemorative game you play?" Bob asked. "A reenactment of rounders?"

"Maybe it's an old-timers' game," Cathy added, laughing. "A really old-timers' game."

"No," Taylor repeated. "I've played rounders."

"Anyway," Bob said, "Cathy and I are big baseball fans."

"But we cheer for different teams," Cathy clarified.

Popping sounds came from the back of the motorhome, ending the baseball talk.

"That's our daughter," Cathy said. "She pops her gum."

"I see," Taylor said.

Taylor had been in the motorhome for a while now, and they'd passed through several towns. He could see parts of the towns that were lit, and the buildings were clearly different from those of his time. After a while, they passed a sign welcoming them to West Virginia. "What is this West Virginia?" he asked.

"West Virginia separated from Virginia during the Civil War," Cathy explained.

It was cozy in the motorhome, gliding along the highway in the dark of night. They reached Parkersburg and then crossed the Ohio River.

"Do you know the Cumberland Road?" Taylor asked.

"I'm sure it was mentioned in a history class," Bob said.

"It connects the Potomac and Ohio Rivers, through the mountains," Taylor said.

When they'd traveled deeper into Ohio, he said, "We're up north now. We've crossed the Mason-Dixon Line."

Soon Bob pulled into a large clearing––a sign had advertised an "RV Park"––and they slept the rest of the night in the motorhome. The next morning the Larkins treated Taylor to a café breakfast before they started out for

Chicago. They got a late start but made good time, passing Akron and Cleveland, and were well across northern Ohio by early afternoon. The kids read and played video games in the back while Bob and Cathy chatted up front. Taylor sat quietly, looking out at the passing countryside, studying the crops and livestock, wondering who ate all the food that was being produced.

"Do you know Mr. Jefferson?" Taylor asked.

"Of course," Bob said. "Thomas Jefferson was our third president."

"He wrote the Declaration of Independence," Cathy added.

"Mr. Jefferson is settled into his home at Monticello now," Taylor said.

"Like now?" Cathy asked.

"I saw Mr. Jefferson once," Taylor continued. "It was on the road. He was alone, riding horseback."

At this, the Larkins' eyes met again, and Chris looked up from his book. Only the chatter of the two kids in back broke the uneasy silence.

"Didn't Jefferson die in the 1820s?" Bob asked.

"Is that so?" Taylor asked.

"Yes. I think it was the 1820s," Bob said.

Taylor moved uncomfortably in his seat, trying to comprehend what Bob had said, that Mr. Jefferson was dead. Taylor summoned the courage and pointed to a calendar on the wall. He'd studied the calendar on a stop to buy gasoline.

"Is that the current calendar?" he asked.

"Yes," Chris said.

"So the year is 1998?"

"Yes."

"Is it not 1821?"

"No sir," Chris said. "It's 1998."

"Is this a joke?" Taylor asked. "Some Halloween prank?"

"No sir, it is not."

"I see," Taylor said slowly.

All the previous night, sleeping uncomfortably in the reclining front seat of the motorhome, Taylor had awakened repeatedly, thinking about what had happened to him. Now he knew. He'd been thrown forward 177 years.

Taylor had never thought much about the future. Now he was in it. His family, his life, had been abruptly taken from him. That was bad enough, but he was homeless and knew nobody in this new world except the Larkins, and he barely knew them. He had no money—no modern money, anyway. He only had some bills and coins from his time. He could already sense the importance of money in the modern world. Of course money talked in his world of 1821, but most people lived on farms and were more self-sufficient, at least able to provide much of their own food.

Above all, there was the sad thought that Taylor's new situation might be permanent and he might never see Ann and the children again. So he gazed at the passing countryside, at the cows and the corn and the wheat, wondering how he might survive in this new world.

⚬◆━━◆▶✕◀◆━━◆⚬

Cathy had been driving for a while when she steered the motorhome into a rest area. She found a parking place. The kids jumped out, and Bob showed Taylor the motorhome's engine. Then Cathy led her husband to a path that wound back into the trees. It was time to talk.

"What is it with this guy?" Cathy asked. "He hasn't heard of Chicago, and he's seen Thomas Jefferson on horseback."

"And he didn't know about baseball," Bob added, "but he's played rounders."

"Bob, how old is Chicago?"

"Eighteen-thirties, I think," Bob said, "chartered in the eighteen-thirties."

"Do you think that's why Mr. Taylor hadn't heard of Chicago, because it didn't exist in his time?" Cathy asked. "Do you really think he could be from two centuries ago? How is that possible?"

"I doubt it," Bob said. "I really doubt it, but who knows?"

"Sometimes I think anything is possible. I'm sure there's a lot goes on that we don't know about. After all, we inhabit and know only a tiny speck of it all."

"So you think the guy's really seen Jefferson?" Cathy asked.

"If I had to bet, I'd say the guy is putting us on. It's a Halloween thing. He's done his homework. He knows a lot about back in those days, and he plays the role really well."

"Yeah, I agree," Cathy said, "and he needed a ride west. Still, there's something different about him."

Bob laughed. "I'm sure he's wary of us too."

"Should we still help him out?" Cathy asked.

"Yes."

They crossed the border into Indiana, and Taylor still dwelled on his predicament, wondering what to do when the Larkins left him off somewhere in Chicago. His options were few.

He knew he had to take advantage of opportunities that came up, just as he'd accepted the ride with the Larkins. He also knew that he had to be careful. How would people treat him if they thought he was from another time? The problem was that it was only natural for him to talk of his life in 1821. That was all he knew, except for the tiny slice of time he'd now spent in 1998.

Every word he spoke, every decision he made, would have consequences, maybe even serious consequences. He would have to be careful. Other people he met might not be as decent as the Larkins.

It was well after dark when they reached the outskirts of Chicago, and the downtown lights beckoned across Lake Michigan.

"Are those buildings?" Taylor asked.

"Yes," Bob said. "Of course."

"How far away are they?"

"Maybe thirty miles," Bob said. "As the crow flies."

Taylor had just learned of Chicago's existence; now he saw it lit up brightly in the distance on a November night.

As they came closer to the city, Bob said, "We're going farther, so we'll drop you off at a hotel downtown. You can spend the night and decide what you want to do."

"But I don't have money for a hotel," Taylor protested, pulling some bills from his pocket. "I only have these and a few silver dollars."

Bob and Cathy got a good look at the funny-looking bills. "Your silver dollars might be worth something," Cathy said.

That made Taylor think of something. He had tried to buy peanuts on a stop for gas, but the clerk wouldn't take his paper money. However, the clerk's face brightened when Taylor pulled out a silver dollar. Taylor got his peanuts, and the clerk got his silver dollar.

"We've put some clothes in a duffel bag," Cathy said. "You'll need them. We hope they'll fit or come close. I've packed some sandwiches too. And you can take the sleeping bag."

Bob reached into his shirt pocket, pulled out a wad of bills, and handed it to Taylor. "Here's something to keep you going for a while," Bob said. It was three hundred dollars.

"I thank you very much for your generosity," Taylor said. "I wouldn't accept this money except that I'm in a difficult situation."

Soon they were in the great city, in the fast-moving traffic. When they reached downtown, Bob pulled up in front of a hotel.

"I wish we could have taken you to a baseball game," Cathy said. "But the season's over."

"I would have liked that, Mrs. Larkin," Taylor said.

Bob and Cathy stepped out of the motorhome to say goodbye. Cathy approached Taylor with her arms wide, saying, "I want to give you a big hug." Taylor blushed.

Bob shook his hand. "Mr. Taylor, I wish you good luck."

"I thank you, sir," Taylor said. "And I thank you, Mrs. Larkin. You've both been very kind to me and you did not have to be. May God bless you and your family."

Taylor's heart sank as the Larkins drove off. He was alone now, in a city whose size he never could have imagined. He had a duffel bag full of clothes, a small sack of food, a sleeping bag, three hundred dollars, and the clothes on his back.

A gust of wind sent a shiver through Taylor. He headed for the hotel entrance. People moved in and out with determined steps. Inside, the lobby was imposing. Guests sat, scattered on comfortable chairs and sofas, reading, talking, and staring into lighted rectangular objects as they rapidly moved their fingers.

Taylor felt better now, welcomed by the big hotel. He walked over to where people were paying for rooms and stepped up to the counter.

"Can I help you, sir?" a clerk asked.

"I would like a room," Taylor said.

"For one?" the clerk asked, taking a long look at Taylor's clothes.

"Yes."

"I have a single room on the eighth floor, for one night," the clerk said.

Taylor carefully unfolded his money and paid the clerk. The clerk gave Taylor a keyed card, directed him to the elevators, and said, "There's a breakfast buffet, Mr. Taylor, served from six to noon."

"Thank you."

"Thank you, Mr. Taylor."

Taylor walked toward the elevators and glanced back. The clerk's head was turned to his colleague. Taylor read his lips, "Did you see that guy's clothes?" the clerk asked.

Taylor joined other guests waiting for an elevator. He noticed how tall people were in 1998. Women seemed to be as tall as men were in his time. There was a *ping*, and an elevator door bolted open. He stepped in after the others and watched as they pushed numbered buttons, which then lit up. He pushed button eight. The elevator rose, and he felt a funny sensation in his stomach.

He found his room and fell onto the bed and slept. When he woke up, he figured out the shower and took a long hot one. Then he did an inventory of the clothes in the duffel bag. There were a pair of casual pants and blue jeans, two shirts, underwear, socks, a belt, a warm jacket, and a baseball cap. He changed into the new clothes. The trousers were too big, but with the belt, it worked. He put on his own boots, from 1821, and then checked himself out in the mirror.

He sat on the bed and ate two ham sandwiches and a small bag of potato chips. Then he drank a soda pop. The fizz burned his throat. He went down to the hotel lobby, found the lounge, and took a seat at the bar. He was immediately drawn to the television above the bar. It was tuned to a football game. Taylor had seen televisions on the trip west, in gas stations and restaurants, but hadn't been able to watch.

The bartender was drying a mug, thoroughly. "What'll ya have?" he asked.

"A beer, please."

"Which one?"

Taylor nodded toward the draft beer handles and said, "One of those."

The action on the screen captivated Taylor. The game was a replay from the previous day. Players with heavy clothing and helmets ran after and hit other players. One player on each team often threw an oblong-shaped ball, and other players tried to catch it. Sometimes a player kicked the ball.

The bartender looked up at the television. "I've always liked the college game," he said.

"This is a college game?" Taylor asked.

"Yeah."

"It's a rough game, isn't it?" Taylor said.

"It is," the bartender said, "but the players have helmets, shoulder pads, and other protection. Aren't you familiar with football?"

Taylor hesitated, sipped some beer, and said, "No, I am not."

"Are you from Europe?"

"I'm from back east," Taylor said. "From the South, actually."

"Well, there's plenty of football down south."

"I see," Taylor said.

Taylor finished his beer, paid, and left a tip. The Larkins had explained tipping to him. He went outside for a walk. A cold, biting wind whipped through the downtown canyons. It was after midnight, long after he and Ann normally went to bed. In the big city, there was night light everywhere. It was lit up like day in some places.

He rose early the next morning. He studied the toothbrush and toothpaste the Larkins put in the duffel bag. He got the hint. He remembered Cathy's disapproving glances at his yellowing teeth.

Taylor carefully brushed his teeth and then put on his new clothes again. He packed his old clothes, from 1821, in the duffel bag. He would not wear the old clothes now. Taylor noticed the previous evening how much better he blended in wearing the new clothes. People didn't look at him the way they had when he wore his old clothes on the drive across the country.

He rode the elevator downstairs to inspect the buffet. He'd never seen such a feast. There were several tables filled with virtually every breakfast food one could imagine. There was bacon, ham, Canadian bacon, sausage, steak, biscuits and gravy, breads, rolls, sweet rolls, donuts, fruit, juices, coffee, and tea. There were eggs that were fried, scrambled, boiled and poached. And this was just breakfast.

Taylor paid the cashier, filled his plate, and ate heartily. He devoured two plates more and washed it all down with orange, tomato, and cranberry juice. Then he feasted on oranges and grapefruit, apples and pears, and drank several cups of coffee.

Taylor knew well that it wasn't polite to eat so much, but he was hungry and didn't know when he would be able to eat like this again. And now his clothes fit better.

Taylor met an older couple at breakfast who suggested some sights to see. There was plenty of time before he had to check out of the hotel, so he ventured out into the brisk morning, wearing his baseball cap. He had seen many people wearing similar billed caps, or some version of the hat, and it suited him too.

He visited a big store just as it opened. There was abundant clothing of all kinds, and televisions and other electronic devices whose function Taylor could only guess. Upon leaving the store, he stepped into the street without looking, and a car slammed to a halt a few feet from him. The driver honked the horn wildly and screamed into the windshield.

Though shaken, Taylor continued on to visit a museum where he spent an hour looking at the paintings, but the biggest thrill was to come. He proceeded up a busy, noisy street into gusts of wind. After walking some blocks, there it was, a building rising to the sky. It was a skyscraper, many times taller than any building he had ever seen. He wondered how it was built and how it stood.

Taylor went inside and boarded an elevator. The elevator shot up, taking his stomach with it. His ears popped, and a woman offered him a stick of chewing gum. The elevator began a long slowdown before finally coming to a stop. There was a restaurant near the top, and Taylor took a seat next to the glass outside wall and ordered a pot of tea.

What a view it was, even better than the view on his favorite mountaintop back home. The giant building was near the blue waters of Lake Michigan. Off to the southeast was the lake's southern shore, where he and the Larkins had passed the night before. In other directions there were more tall buildings, some of them also skyscrapers. Chicago was fantastically big, dwarfing the biggest cities he had seen in his time.

He only had to lean in his chair toward the glass wall, which separated him from the abyss, and he became dizzy. He lingered over his tea, enjoying the vertical experience, finally returning to the hotel to gather his things and check out. He waited in the lobby for the elderly couple who'd offered him a ride west. Taylor was ready to get out of the city. The big city was impressive, but it overwhelmed him.

The woman arrived and led Taylor outside where her husband waited in an older vehicle. He slipped into the back seat of the warm car. The man assured him that he maintained the car and changed the oil regularly. The couple was returning home to the northern prairie after a visit to the big city.

The man expertly guided the big car out of the city. They passed mile after mile of houses and buildings, and Taylor thought how it had all once been farmland.

Finally, they reached the open prairie. The fields were lush. Taylor had wondered who ate all the food that was being produced in modern America. Now he knew. He'd seen Chicago, and there were many other big cities with millions of people in the country now, from the Atlantic to the Pacific. The Larkins had shown him on a map in their travel atlas.

The older couple didn't ask Taylor many questions, nor did they talk much. They reached the Mississippi by midafternoon. The man steered the car down to the river. Taylor got out and walked to the river's edge. He knew rivers and could see that this river was a powerful one. He was amazed at all the water that flowed before him. He thought of all the little streams that fed this great river.

Taylor thought of how back in his time the Mississippi flowed on the western edge of the country, and there were French settlements along the river from St. Louis to

New Orleans. Most goods moved on water then, and the Mississippi pulled goods south to the Gulf.

Soon they were back on the highway, heading west. Taylor had never seen such a vast prairie. The land rolled and rolled, and rolled on some more. The woman pressed something and suddenly there was music. A bard sang of lost love. Then two northern girls sang. Their voices were strong and clear.

After a while, the man pulled the car off the four-lane. The couple treated Taylor to a hamburger at a small restaurant. He wasn't that hungry after his big breakfast at the hotel, but he ate anyway. They sat outdoors at a picnic table and ate their hamburgers, and the man explained hitchhiking.

"When a car approaches, you extend your arm and stick up your thumb," the man said, as he demonstrated. Taylor did the same, copying the man.

They traveled a bit farther before leaving the road again. The man stopped at the end of the exit ramp. "We're heading north," the man said. "We have to let you off here."

Taylor thanked the couple and climbed out of the car. It was close to dusk, so he decided to take cover for the night. He walked north on the two-lane road, studying the cornfields on both sides. The corn was dry and tan-colored, ready to be harvested. This would be where he would sleep tonight.

Taylor knew he had to be careful. The farmer would be protective of his land, and there was a farmyard just a half-mile up the road. The farmyard was surrounded by a tree break, a mix of deciduous and pine trees. He waited until there were no cars and then sprinted the short distance across the grassy roadside to the cornfield. He dropped his bags over the fence, parted the wires and crawled through, carefully avoiding the sharp prongs. Then he disappeared into the corn.

Taking no chances, Taylor walked deep into the field, brushing against the long corn leaves before finding the right spot. He tore off some leaves to sit on and ate his last sandwich, then buried himself in the sleeping bag. Sleep would be a relief. He said a prayer and soon dozed off, despite the noisy chorus of scraping corn leaves.

He awakened at first light. The wind had calmed, and the corn was nearly silent. He was surprised how warm the sleeping bag had kept him. He remained burrowed in the bag for a long time, wary of the cold jolt that awaited him, and plotted the day ahead. Reality was closing in again. His food was gone, and $150 was left in his pocket.

Taylor organized his things and went to the edge of the field. A pickup truck had just passed and Taylor jumped back into the corn. He'd learned about rearview mirrors. He looked again. The road was clear. He climbed between the fence wires, stepped up to the road, set up on the on-ramp, and waited for a ride. Taylor stuck out his thumb when a vehicle passed, but few passed.

After a couple sped by on a motorcycle, Taylor moved farther down the ramp, where travelers on the four-lane could see him. Soon, a farmer came down the ramp and stopped. The farmer drove Taylor to the next exit where there was a gas station and truckers buying gas. "Truckers aren't supposed to give rides," the man explained, "but some do anyway. They want to talk, to stay awake."

The farmer was right. Before long, a big truck, making grinding and gasping sounds, slowed, then stopped on the on-ramp. Taylor hustled to the truck. The passenger door opened. The driver was a big blond guy and wore a billed cap with the logo of his favorite rock band.

"Where ya headed?" the trucker asked.

"West."

"Get in."

Taylor climbed up into a big, comfortable seat.

"How far west ya going?" the trucker asked.

"I'm not sure."

"Would ya like some hot tea?"

"Sure."

The trucker handed Taylor a big thermos. "It's easier if ya pour it yourself," he said. "The cup's clean, I promise."

"Thank you, sir," Taylor said as he poured a cup. "I'll gladly have tea. You know tea was difficult to buy during the Revolutionary War. It was scarce."

"Is that so?"

"How far are you traveling?" Taylor asked.

"Colorado, then Utah."

Colorado. Utah. The words sounded exotic to Taylor.

"Are those cities?" Taylor asked.

"States," the trucker said. "They're states."

"Have you ever been to California?" Taylor asked.

"Yeah."

"California was under Spanish rule," Taylor said. "But I think it's under Mexico now."

"Not now, my friend," the trucker said. "California's a state in the USA."

"So California is a state now?"

"You bet," the trucker said. "Didn't you know that?"

"I did not," Taylor caught the trucker's puzzled look. "I've read that California is a sunny place."

"Nice weather," the trucker said, "but there's lots of people out there. I prefer the wide-open spaces."

It was a fine day on the prairie, sunny and warm, though there was a feeling of finality, for such nice days were numbered now, before the crush of winter's cold.

Taylor had a good view from his perch in the truck's cabin. The agricultural bounty didn't seem to end. The driver pointed to a field and said, "It looks like most of the soybeans have been harvested by now. Makes sense. It's early November."

"Soybeans?"

"They're fed to cattle and hogs. People eat them too." He handed Taylor a bag of what looked like small brown nuts. "Try some."

Taylor did. The soybeans were crunchy and had a nutty taste.

"Soybeans are exported too," the trucker said, "especially to Asia."

Much of the corn had also been harvested, and cattle grazed in the harvested fields. "There's a lot of that fence," Taylor said, pointing to the side of the highway.

"That's barbwire," the trucker said.

"Is that what it's called?"

"Yep, invented last century," the trucker said. "Barbwire really changed things out west."

They passed farmyards too, where the farmers who produced all the food lived. The farmyards were clean and orderly, with nice houses and substantial outbuildings. And there were some older red barns too. But Taylor missed trees. There weren't many trees compared to back east where he was from. On the prairie, trees grew along the creeks, around farmyards and between fields, but mostly it was open country.

"See the combine?" the trucker asked, pointing to a great cloud of dust where a huge machine moved through a cornfield. The combine was near the road, so Taylor got a good look.

"It's big, really big," Taylor said. "I'm still getting used to all these machines."

Once again, the trucker had a puzzled look. "You don't have such big harvesters back where you come from?" he asked.

"No," Taylor said. "Are the brown cattle Herefords?"

"Yep."

"Herefords were recently brought to the country, from Great Britain," Taylor said.

"What?" the trucker protested. "I've seen Hereford cattle all my life."

"I don't doubt that," Taylor said.

"Which crops do you grow back where you live?" the trucker asked.

"Tobacco, corn, wheat," Taylor said.

It was late afternoon when the trucker pulled the big truck into a rest area. "I've got to stop here," he said. "I hardly slept last night, and coffee keeps a fella going only so long. I hate to miss the rest of this beautiful day, but I've got to sleep.

"Let me warn you," the man continued, "it may be beautiful now, but weather changes fast here on the prairie, and there's a cold front moving in. Temperatures are supposed to really drop. It might even snow.

"You should be able to get another ride here," the trucker said, as he stopped the rig in a row of trucks. "If you don't travel on tonight, there's a park up the road. It has cabins and a restaurant. Maybe you can get a warm meal. You might need it."

"That sounds good," Taylor said. "I've traveled a long way."

"You might even want to land here for a while," the trucker said. "People are decent in these parts."

"I thank you, sir, for the ride and for your counsel," Taylor said, before climbing down from the cabin. "And I thank you for the giant sandwich."

"Good luck to you," the trucker said.

Taylor walked away from the long line of trucks, many with engines running, the drivers resting from long hauls across the country. He crossed over to a grassy area with picnic tables, stretched his arms, and breathed the fresh air. Off to the west, a sinking sun shone on the prairie. There was a stand of trees down below, across a gravel road. The trees had lost most of their leaves, but red, orange, and yellow leaves were still vivid among the browns and tans of late autumn. The bright colors had reigned only a short time before.

Taylor sat down and soaked up the last of the day's warmth. He pulled the footlong from his duffel bag. The sandwich was loaded with beef and vegetables. He intended to eat only half, but he couldn't stop. He was hungry, and the sandwich was delicious.

After the meal, he stretched out on the long seat of the picnic table, exhausted. He'd been away from home for three days now, and much had happened. His life had changed in a way he never could have imagined. The warmth of the waning sun gently pricked his face as his mind moved in and out of consciousness. Finally, he drifted off.

When Taylor awakened, the sun was setting. The temperature had fallen and would drop more in minutes when the great fireball fell over the edge of the prairie. The gravel road below paralleled the four-lane highway and led to where Taylor wanted to go. He grabbed his bags and climbed down the hillside to the road. The road was little used and was lined in places with sumac bushes, a few still bright red. There was a cabin back among the trees, and Taylor spotted a deer. After a couple miles, the country road rose up to meet a paved road, and Taylor turned in the direction of the park. Darkness was gathering. He walked faster.

After an hour he reached a narrow road lined with trees, which led to the park. He was energized by the hike and could feel his leg muscles stretch. He passed the entrance and approached the park office. It was closed. There would be no cozy cabin tonight. Taylor's options had narrowed again. He was without shelter and food, and his dwindling stash of cash was no help to him now. The temperature was plummeting, and the wind was beginning to howl.

Taylor zipped his jacket to the top against the cold and walked down a hill and back up another, passing the closed restaurant and darkened cabins. The park was empty. The wind was growing fierce, as was the sound of blowing leaves scraping the ground.

Taylor saw a light. It was a bathroom. Better yet, the bathroom was still warm from the day's sun. Taylor washed his hands and splashed warm water on his face. Then he walked down another hill lined with more dark cabins and retrieved the flashlight the trucker had given him. At the bottom of the hill, he found a picnic table under an open shelter that was ringed by bushes.

What luck! Tonight Taylor would be off the ground and protected from rain and snow. He laid out the sleeping bag on the table, took off his boots, quickly got in, zipped the bag, and pulled it over his head. As the wind howled in the trees, Taylor gave thanks for the help he'd been given on his trip west. He didn't know the people who'd given him rides and food and money. They'd helped him for no other reason than that they were fellow travelers on life's road.

Taylor thought how his father read stories to him and the other children before they slept, tales about knights of old who protected women and the poor. Now it was he who slept outdoors in winter's first blast, with little money and no food.

Taylor woke the next morning to a silvery wonderland. It hadn't snowed, but frost was all around. Frost covered the ground and clung to the trees. Taylor was frozen. He hadn't thought it would get so cold. The sleeping bag had kept him alive, but it hadn't kept him warm. He awakened repeatedly through the night to the wind sucking warmth from his body. It was the howl of a cold front whipping across the prairie. There was little to slow it, no mountains or forests, as it barreled down from the north. And Taylor could sense there was worse to come.

He gathered his things and ran up the hill to the bathroom. The bathroom was heated, and it felt good. He ran warm water over his hands and wrists and washed his numb face with the washcloth Cathy had put in the duffel bag. Then he moved on to the hand dryer, pushing the start button over and over, the warm air warming him more and more. *What an invention,* he marveled.

Taylor hoofed it to the park restaurant. It was still closed. A woman unlocked the door. "We open at eleven," she said.

He thanked the woman and walked to the park office. The clerk thought it odd that he didn't have a car but let him have a cabin anyway. When he got to the cabin, Taylor sat in front of the electric heater and read a newsmagazine left there.

At noon, he returned to the restaurant. The small dining room was quiet. He ordered the daily special, white beans over corn bread, and asked the waitress, Joni, about work in the area. Joni told him that sometimes the manager let people work for meals. The manager came to Taylor's table and told him he could wash dishes for his lunch and could do the same for his evening meal. Taylor drank another cup of coffee and got to work washing dishes.

He was back at the restaurant the next day eating a hamburger and then scrubbing pots and pans. After lunch, when work was caught up, he took a seat at the staff table, near the entrance to the kitchen. Joni joined him at the table. She wore her blonde hair pulled tight in a ponytail, which accentuated her oval face. Joni told Taylor her story. She was the single mom of a young boy. Then she said, "If you're needing a job, Mr. Taylor, my brother knows a farm family that needs a hired hand. The farm is about five miles from here."

"I surely could use the work," Taylor said.

"Have you done farm work before?"

"As a younger man I did."

"Around here?"

"It was back east," he said.

"That's a long ways away," Joni said. "If you're down on your luck, this job might just be the right thing for you. My brother knows the family, the Smiths, Carl and Doris. He says they're good people. They treat their hired man well. And there's a house that comes with the job. I have the day off tomorrow. I can take you there if you want."

"Thanks," Taylor said. "I would appreciate that a lot."

"You look like a decent guy," Joni said. "If you're there on the spot, maybe they'll hire you right away. One in the hand is worth two in the bush, right? But you'll want to be honest with them about not knowing how to drive."

"I will," he said.

"You'll learn to drive," Joni said. "It's easy."

Taylor stood up to return to the kitchen, and Joni stared at his boots. "I like your boots, Mr. Taylor. They're old-fashioned, really retro. They're cool."

He smiled. "Thanks, Joni."

Joni arrived early the next morning to pick up Taylor. Her son was strapped in a small seat in the back seat of the car. Joni drove the back roads, the gravel roads, to the Smith farm. When she dropped Taylor off, he handed her a twenty-dollar bill. "For gas," he said. It was about the last of the money the Larkins had given him.

"You don't have to do that, Mr. Taylor," she protested. But her resistance didn't last, and she took the money. She had a boy to feed.

As Joni drove off, Carl pulled up in a pickup truck, introduced himself, and took Taylor on a tour of the farm. Carl showed Taylor the cattle and the corn that hadn't been harvested yet. Carl had already finished cutting the soybeans. When they returned to the farmyard, Carl showed Taylor the machinery and the outbuildings. It was clear that the Smiths ran an efficient operation.

As Carl closed the barn door, he said, "The kids are raised, and not one of them wanted to stay on the farm. Doris and I are alone here now."

He got to the point. "I heard you've done farmwork before."

"I grew up on a farm."

"I also heard that you don't drive," Carl said.

"I haven't had the chance to drive," Taylor answered calmly. "We used draft animals on the farm where I worked."

"Draft animals?" There was suspicion in Carl's voice. "You cultivated with draft animals?"

"Yes."

"You're not one of these people who's opposed to using modern machinery are you?" Carl asked. "Opposed to modern farming methods?"

"No, sir," Taylor said. "I am not."

"Good," Carl said. "I want you to know that we practice progressive farming methods on our farm."

"I understand, sir."

"We pay our hired man seven dollars an hour. That's well above the minimum wage," Carl explained. "But I can't offer you full-time work all the time. Sometimes it will be full time. Sometimes it won't. But it'll always be at least thirty hours a week. You can count on that." Carl said it in a way that Taylor knew he could trust him.

They walked toward a small house at the other end of the farmyard. "We built this little house for Doris's mother when Grandpa died," Carl said. "Grandma lived here for fifteen years until she passed. Grandma always called it the little house, and the name stuck. But it's been empty a lot since she died. "You can stay here, as long as you pay the gas and electricity and help maintain it."

The little house had an empty-house smell. It was simply furnished but was cozy.

"It's not a bad place," Carl said. "Has all you need." Taylor nodded in agreement.

"We keep a garden in summer," Carl continued, "and have lots of fresh vegetables, and we have a small orchard out back. So you'll have a roof over your head, food to eat, and money in your pocket. Seems to me you'll be set."

"Yes, I will," Taylor said, more thrilled than he let on.

He promptly got started setting up in his little home. He had few possessions, so moving in was easy. However, the place needed a good cleaning. Taylor dusted, vacuumed, and washed windows. And he had to learn how things worked, about appliances and electronics that were new to him, such as the refrigerator, washing machine, and DVD player.

Carl gave Taylor a pay advance and drove him to town to buy groceries. Taylor also bought pants, jeans, gloves, socks, and work boots. Carl had already given him a warm coat and two new seed-corn hats, still another variety of the billed cap he had seen everywhere.

Taylor started work the next day. He and Carl checked the cattle, windmills, and water tanks. The cattle were mostly

Herefords, the brown ones like those Taylor had seen on his trip west. Carl showed him how to fix barbwire fence, repeatedly warning him of its danger. It was a gray but calm November day, a day still warm enough for painting, so that afternoon they got started on the barn. It felt good to be working and earning money again.

The next day they painted and then went to the courthouse to get Taylor a driver's permit. That afternoon Taylor got his first driving lesson. They took the old pickup truck out to the pasture. It was bumpy riding, but Taylor caught on fast. The truck had a manual transmission, a stick shift on the floor, and there was a lot of grinding when Taylor shifted. Otherwise, things went well.

Taylor soon drove on gravel roads and, before long, was a competent, licensed driver. Carl told him the truck was his to use as long as he maintained it.

<hr>

As November passed, so did the last of autumn's bright colors. Yet there was still beautiful color, especially when the late afternoon sun shone on the browns and tans, creating a golden hue.

Soon it was Thanksgiving, and the Smith family gathered. Two of the kids lived nearby and arrived with their spouses and kids. Taylor did chores in the morning; then he cleaned up and joined the family for turkey dinner. Each person, including the kids, gave thanks before the meal.

Taylor gave thanks for the job and house the Smiths had provided him. He also expressed gratitude for the plenty of modern America, something he was still getting used to.

Then the questions started, directed to Taylor. "Do you eat turkey on Thanksgiving where you come from?" a grandchild asked.

"Yes," Taylor answered, "and some eat ham too."

The turkey was moist, and the mashed potatoes with gravy made Taylor's mouth tingle. He ate two plates full.

The questions continued. The Smith family was curious about Taylor but wary. Taylor saw that the whole family had been well briefed about him, done with the same efficiency as they did everything else.

"We took Mr. Taylor to church last Sunday," Carl said. "To our church."

"But I think Mr. Taylor wants to go to his church," Doris added, as she served pumpkin pie. "And we've found a church for him. He'll attend services there this coming Sunday."

The celebration broke up early evening, and all the guests took food home. Taylor was learning the effect of all the new machines and the new technology, such as the telephone and email, which had come into use since his time. And the talk moved incredibly fast. The new technology sped up all that passed between the human lips.

Radio and television amplified talk on a grander scale. The result was that there was talk, talk, talk, and more talk.

The week after Thanksgiving cold air came down from Canada and snuffed out the last life of autumn. Geese sped south, squawking as if fleeing something horrible. The cold came in waves, like a conquering army. It advanced, retreated, and then returned again in ever-colder assaults.

Taylor sat evenings close to the woodstove, grateful to have shelter from the cold. The crackling fire was reassuring, just as it was back home when the family gathered around the fireplace. Taylor had plenty of wood. He'd gathered a winter's supply for his little house and for Carl and Doris from dead trees along the creek that ran through the big pasture.

In December, Taylor sent three hundred dollars to Bob and Cathy Larkin. The local librarian helped him find their address and phone number.

On a bitterly cold night in January, Taylor crossed the farmyard to the Smith house. It was deep winter now. The biting wind seemed to blow right through him. The wind took his breath away. The light in the house windows was inviting in the frozen darkness.

Doris had invited Taylor to supper. She'd made a big pot of stew, and it was more than she and Carl could eat, she kept saying. There was homemade bread and salad too. After dessert, Carl said, "Mr. Taylor, come take a look. There's a television program on tonight I think you might like to watch."

They took their coffee into the living room. The program had just begun. The music pulled Taylor in immediately. It

44

was more like music from his time. The documentary was about a pivotal battle during the Civil War. The battle was called Gettysburg.

By the time the show ended, Taylor learned about the epic battle that lasted three days in early July 1863. He learned about Confederate General Robert E. Lee's Army of Northern Virginia and Union General George Meade's Army of the Potomac, about the fight in the peach orchard, and about Confederate General Pickett's charge to try to capture Cemetery Ridge on the final day of the battle. And he learned about the awful carnage.

After the program, Taylor sat, stunned, in his chair, color drained from his face.

"Are you all right, Mr. Taylor?" Doris asked.

"Yes," he answered weakly.

"But you don't look so good," she said.

"I think I'll go back to my house."

Doris went to the kitchen and cut a big piece of chocolate cake, put it in a plastic container, and handed it to Taylor.

"Thanks," Taylor said. "Good night, Doris. Good night, Carl." He opened the door to leave and a cold blast sucked warmth from the kitchen.

He stayed up into the early morning, sitting next to the woodstove, thinking about Gettysburg. In his time, 1821, Taylor knew of the growing tension between northern and southern states, but he didn't think it would come to civil war. What astonished him was that less than a century after the founding of the country on high ideals, the states fought a horrific war.

Taylor watched the remaining parts of the television series about the Civil War and learned more about the war from encyclopedias kept in his house and from books and DVDs from the library. People from his church also lent him books. Some church members had ancestors who'd fought and died in the Civil War.

Taylor learned about abolitionists and the growing divide between northern and southern states, and the subsequent secession from the Union of eleven southern states to establish the Confederate States of America. And he learned about President Lincoln's Emancipation Proclamation, which freed slaves in the Confederate states, and about the war's end with General Lee's surrender to General Grant at Appomattox. Most disturbing, Taylor learned of the hundreds of thousands of dead and wounded in the conflict, though he could never bring himself to look for lists of war dead.

Taylor learned about much more that had occurred in the 177 years that he'd been propelled forward on the previous Halloween night. He read about the history of flight, and he learned, most incredibly, that American astronauts had visited the moon, only sixty-six years after the Wright brothers' first flight. He learned about Thomas Edison, the civil rights movement, the world wars and the bloody twentieth century, and, most fascinating, the possibility of intelligent life existing out among the stars. Taylor even read law books on weekends at the office of a lawyer friend from church.

In winter, work was more difficult. In fact, everything was harder in the cold. And cold lurked everywhere. Cold sapped one's energy. Doris's arthritis acted up, and Carl's hip hurt more. Taylor wore extra layers, drank coffee, and added wood to the fire, all to get warm and stay warm. Survival was the goal. Survive until spring.

One of Taylor's tasks on the farm was to take care of Mabel, the Smiths' horse. Sometimes he rode Mabel to check the cattle, and they also went on long rides. Riding Mabel lifted Taylor's spirits. He had ridden and cared for horses most of his life.

In late January, Taylor mailed a letter home to his family. He addressed the letter to his wife, care of the local post office. Taylor knew it wasn't logical to try to send a letter through time, but why not try, especially after what had happened to him on Halloween night. However, not long after, Doris gave the returned letter to Taylor.

There'd been snowstorms since Taylor came to the prairie in early November, but the blizzard later that winter was different. The white terror swept across the high plains and on to the prairie. The wind and snow blew across endless fields of corn stubble and pastures inhabited by forlorn, frozen cattle.

The wind howled and made alarming siren sounds. These were frigid blasts that give existential thoughts to even the truest believers. Besides the ceaseless wind, Taylor, warm in his house, heard only the constant rattle of the farmyard light, high on its pole.

He looked out at the tiny snowflakes blowing horizontally under the light. The snow coalesced in ever-changing patterns, before piling up in frozen waves. Taylor wondered how the farmyard squirrels, high up in the trees, were coping in the fierce wind. Would their leafy nests hold?

By morning the snow had stopped, but the wind still raged. Taylor dressed in his warmest layers and ate a big bowl of oatmeal before venturing into the deep freeze. He'd left the pickup in the shed. After some coaxing, the truck started. He left the truck running and returned to the house to fetch a thermos of steaming coffee.

Taylor drove carefully toward the pasture. The wind had blown since the storm began, and there were stretches on the pasture where the snow wasn't deep. Taylor found his way. The cattle were gathered behind the shelter Carl had built down among the cottonwood trees, now barren, not far from the creek. The cattle were in pretty good shape, thanks to the shelter. Taylor broke the ice in the water tank higher up in the pasture so the cattle could drink.

Taylor was nearly frozen. The wind had efficiently stolen warmth from his body. As he drove back to the farmyard, the old pickup's engine truly warmed, and intense heat blew from beneath the dashboard. Back at the house, it took two bowls of piping-hot soup to finally warm him. Then he spread peanut butter and jelly on crackers, eating plenty.

As he often did, Taylor wondered what the cold was like farther north. What was it like up in Canada, and farther up in Canada? Could it really be colder than what he was enduring?

Winter was getting to him. On the Saturday after the blizzard, Taylor rode Mabel to a country tavern late in the afternoon. He called the place a tavern. Only now, in 1999, it was a bar and restaurant.

When he arrived at the restaurant, Taylor tied Mabel to a post and covered her with a blanket. The bar was packed. Others had cabin fever too. He found a place to stand at the bar. The televisions were tuned to college basketball. Standing next to other bar patrons, Taylor was reminded how tall people were in the modern world, especially on the prairie.

Despite the many weeks of cold, agreeability reigned at the bar. Guys were buying drinks. Alcohol was loosening pockets. Taylor drank a beer and had a shot of whiskey.

"Aren't you the new guy working for the Smiths?" asked a man standing nearby. "From back east."

"Yes, I am," Taylor answered. He had never met the man, had never seen him. They talked a little weather and some sports.

Taylor didn't stay long but bought a round before riding home in the darkness. It was cold, but thankfully the wind was calm. And it was surprisingly bright, with the moonlight shining on the snowy countryside. It was quiet, very quiet.

He had time to think about things that winter, especially during evenings after supper. He liked his situation with the Smiths and felt lucky to have landed there. However, he hadn't worked for someone for a long time, and sometimes it was difficult. He got to thinking about what it must be like to have most of one's life controlled by others. He thought more about what it was like to be a slave.

Taylor didn't own slaves back in his life in 1821. In fact, he opposed slavery. He simply didn't think it was right for a person to own another human being.

After the revolution against Great Britain, the spirit of freedom was strong in the young country. Some slave owners, in both southern and northern states, freed their slaves. Other slaves bought their freedom. There was a growing number of freed slaves in the upper South. However, over time, that spirit of freedom began to fade.

———◆◆◆◆———

Finally, there was a break in winter. Flocks of robins appeared, and soon after, a stray cat showed up on the farm. Carl found her hunting mice in the barn and hired her immediately. Carl called her Katze, and the name stuck. Mostly, it was Taylor who looked after Katze, feeding and caring for her. Katze holed up in cozy spots around the farmyard, ever on alert for mice.

With spring, Carl and Taylor got started cultivating the fields. In April, Doris started the garden, planting cool weather plants: radishes, spinach, and lettuce. Taylor worked in the garden in the evenings. In May, they planted the hot-weather vegetables: tomatoes, cucumbers, and peppers.

Mostly Doris planted hybrid vegetables, plants developed in modern times. The hybrids grew quickly, produced well, and looked nice. However, Doris also grew heirloom plants. Heirlooms reached back into the distant past. Heirloom vegetables weren't as pretty or productive as the hybrids, but often they tasted better.

Taylor was surprised by the productivity of the hybrid vegetables, especially the tomatoes when they came on in later summer. However, he preferred the heirlooms. They were like the vegetables he grew back home in his time.

Gardening, like farming, was elemental. Taylor was amazed by the process: plant a seed, coax the tiny plant above ground, and then water and nurture it until it yields something delicious. Doris said that growing things gets into your head, like the beat of a good song.

Taylor liked life on the prairie. It was a quiet and simple life. The rhythm of the land still beat in the people of the prairie, reminding them what is possible and what is not.

June came with bright blue skies and streaky clouds and the warmth of early summer. The trees in the Smith farmyard were fully leafed now, and the wind made music in the leaves. Silvery cottonwoods along the creek shimmered in the sun.

One evening the sky darkened in the west. Black clouds swirled, and the temperature dropped sharply. Taylor heard the wind gusts and looked out at the sudden early evening darkness. Soon rain battered his little house, and there was violent thunder and lightning all around. Then someone pounded on his door. It was Doris. "There's a tornado warning," she said. "You'd better come to the storm cellar."

Taylor followed her through the driving rain. The storm was much scarier outdoors. Rain pelted the ground, and lightning cracked as they ran toward Carl, who stood at the cellar entrance holding a muscular flashlight.

Carl bent down and lifted a flat, wooden door that was level to the ground. With his flashlight showing the way, one by one they descended the steps to nowhere, leading to a few square feet of earthen floor. Carl closed the door above them and pulled a small radio from his pocket, tuning it to a broadcast covering the weather threat.

They stayed in the shelter for an hour, rain slamming the door above them. When they stepped outside, light had returned. All was calm. A tornado hadn't materialized. The storm had passed, moving to the east to threaten others. And lighting bugs once again flashed green across the farmyard.

It wasn't long after the storm that Taylor found his duffel bag unzipped. He kept the bag in his closet. It contained his clothes from his time, those he wore when he stepped into 1998. He was sure the bag had been fully zipped, and he wondered if the neatly packed clothes were now ruffled.

Hot summer came by late June, and huge puffy clouds cast giant shadows on the land. With the heat came the cicadas' song. It was a chorus, and they sang into the evening.

Taylor had followed the sports teams since arriving on the Smith farm. However, in summer he mostly followed baseball. He went to a few town ball games with Carl and Doris and watched Saturday games on television.

Often on sultry nights, Taylor drove the old pickup to the high point of the big pasture and tuned to games on the radio. There was usually static, so he adjusted the dial to find the broadcast with the best reception. Despite the static, the announcer's voice, the crack of the bat, and the crowd's roar were summertime balm for a man missing home and family.

As much as Taylor loved baseball, some things in the modern world disturbed him, and much of what disturbed him came to him on television. Sometimes he couldn't believe what he was seeing or hearing. Yet he saw the remarkable power of television, where the latest thing surged through the country like a thunderbolt.

What he saw on television was mostly far away. Life around him was quiet and peaceful. Most unpleasant noise he heard was from the farm machinery or the few vehicles passing along the gravel road. It was a vast country, a continental country. There was plenty of room.

Taylor often wondered what Mr. Jefferson would think of the modern world. What would Jefferson think of so many Americans living in crowded cities? What would he think of all the new technology and its incredible power? Surely, Taylor thought, Mr. Jefferson would not approve.

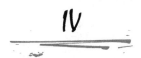

IV

In September, cool air came down from Canada and drove out the heat and humidity of summer, breathing new life into the sunbaked prairie. Balmy days followed, days with perfect temperatures and Mediterranean-blue skies. These were calm days whose only disturbance was the fading buzz of insects, the autumn beauty more compelling because of the winter to come. On one of these golden days, squirrels frolicked in the farmyard, efficiently devouring acorns. A fox, not more than twenty feet from Taylor, sauntered across the farmyard. Their eyes locked. The fox's gaze was intelligent, even having a look of awareness.

One day at dusk, Taylor rode Mabel out to the four-lane highway. He tied her to a fence post, walked up the embankment to the highway, and watched the traffic speeding past. After a while, he stepped back down the embankment and stroked Mabel, still watching the passing vehicles.

Two more times Taylor made the same reconnaissance ride to the four-lane. On October 29, with ghosts and goblins occupying the Smith front lawn, Taylor paid a visit to Doris and Carl. It was evening, and the couple lingered over coffee at the kitchen table. Taylor had already given his two-week notice.

"We're sorry to see you go," Carl said. "I know hired hands don't usually last long, but we wish you could have stayed longer. We'll be all right, though. We've finished cutting the soybeans, and Doris will help with the rest of the corn."

"It's been a year now," Taylor said.

"Sure enough," Carl said. "You came around Halloween last year, didn't you?"

"Are you sure you want to hitchhike?" Doris asked.

"Yes," Taylor said. "It'll be okay."

They chatted a while longer, sharing stories of the previous year, before saying their goodbyes.

Taylor had already withdrawn the money from his account at the town bank and kept only what he needed for his trip. He gave the remainder of the money to his church and to Joni. Taylor hadn't seen Joni since she'd dropped him off at the farm a year earlier. He was grateful to her for helping him land the job with Carl and Doris. And he knew she needed the money. She had a boy to raise.

Taylor returned to the little house, sat down at the kitchen table, and wrote a letter to Carl and Doris. He thanked them for the job, for use of the house and the pickup truck, and for helping him at a difficult time of his life. He paused, looked out the window, and wondered how much more to say. Finally, he wrote:

> I suppose you have wondered about me. Last year, on Halloween night, I was mysteriously, and completely against my will, transported through time from my life in 1821. I know you'll have a hard time believing this, but it's true.

Taylor signed the letter and placed it on the table, anchored by a spoon. Then he made five sandwiches and packed them in the duffel bag with carrots and chips. He tidied up the house, drank some coffee, and studied the perpetual calendar one last time. Then he sat down and thought, focusing on the task before him. And he prayed.

Shortly before midnight, Taylor turned off the lights, locked the door, and placed his two house keys under the porch mat. It was well past the Smiths' bedtime, and the only light came from the farmyard light, high up on its pole. Taylor carried only the duffel and sleeping bags as he crossed the farmyard.

There was a meow in the darkness. It was Katze. She brushed against Taylor's leg. Katze had come to say goodbye.

"I wondered where you were," Taylor whispered, picking her up and petting her. He kissed her on the head and set her down. Katze meowed and meowed. "Ssshh," Taylor pleaded, before petting her again.

Taylor made his way up the road, gravel crunching with each step. It was chilly, even without the breeze. Colder blasts were coming. After an hour, Taylor saw light from the four-lane highway. As he drew closer, he could hear the hum of vehicles in the distance. Soon he heard truck engines grinding.

Taylor reached the four-lane and walked another mile to an on-ramp. Before long, a truck stopped. The ride took him past Chicago, into Indiana. It was morning, and Taylor settled into a café for breakfast.

Things were different from how they were a year earlier when Taylor, taken from his world of 1821 and thrust into the modern world, traveled west to the prairie where he slept in a cornfield. Now he was confidently dressed in modern clothes, wearing jeans, a sweater and jacket, and a seed-corn hat. And now he pounded the road with a pair of handsome walking shoes. Taylor still spoke differently, in an older way, but people thought he was from Europe or something.

Taylor had lived in the modern world for a year now and could talk the talk of 1999. He could chat about sports and news. Now Taylor didn't face the glances, stares, and questions that he had a year earlier on his trip west. He usually fit in now, often wearing some type of baseball cap.

A salesman from a small town stopped next for Taylor. The salesman was returning from a trek up north, where he'd done good business. He was a friendly guy and conversed easily with Taylor as they angled south into central Indiana.

"Have you watched the baseball playoffs?" Taylor asked.

"I've watched some," the salesman answered, "but I'm mostly a Hoosier fan. I cheer for all things Hoosier."

"I've watched the Hoosiers," Taylor said. "And I've usually cheered for them. Indiana was a state in my time."

At this, their hands clapped in a high five. "But my team is Mr. Jefferson's university," Taylor added.

The salesman invited Taylor to stay the night at his house, and he broke bread that evening with the salesman's family and slept on the living room couch.

Early the next morning, the salesman drove Taylor out to the highway. Two rides took him most of the rest of the way, passing through Cincinnati and on through southern Ohio, then across West Virginia. Taylor was making good time, so he stopped for a hamburger and coffee before getting his final ride. When that driver stopped for gas in a small town, it was dusk, and trick-or- treaters were already on the streets in their annual hunt for candy.

When they approached Taylor's town, it was almost dark. However, he knew the area well, the contour and look of the land, and he knew the place where he wanted to get out. He asked the driver to slow down and then stop. The driver guided the car onto the shoulder and turned on the emergency lights. Taylor pulled out most of what remained of his money and handed it to the driver. "For gas," Taylor said.

The driver, a young guy, didn't resist. "Thanks, mister, thanks a lot. Glad I could help you out."

"Thanks for the ride."

He was sure he was near the place where he'd entered 1998, where the Larkins had stopped in their motorhome as trucks sped by, exactly a year earlier. He descended the embankment and crossed a field, softly saying the Lord's Prayer. "Our Father, who art in heaven, hallowed be thy Name ....."

He walked farther and thought he could see the road in the darkness, the dirt road he'd been riding on a year earlier, the road that led to town and home. He drew closer. And there it was. He stepped onto the road. Joy surged through him.

Taylor walked a ways and then slipped into the woods and changed into the clothes he carried in the duffel bag, the shirt, pants, overcoat, boots, and crumpled top hat of 1821. He stuffed his modern clothes into the bag and walked on, fallen leaves crunching under his boots. There was a bonfire back in the woods, and he heard muffled voices and the crackle and pop of the fire. He walked faster, passing farmhouses with dimly lit windows. A rider approached, saying, "Good evening, Mr. Taylor."

He drew nearer to home and was thrilled at the thought of seeing Ann and the children. He saw the outline of fruit trees on the edge of their property. Then he saw light in the house windows. Maybe Ann was still up, reading to the children. Taylor stashed the bags in the barn. He didn't want to have to explain that now. He ran toward the house. Finally, he stood at the door. Ann knew her husband's knock, and she bolted from her chair and rushed to the door.

They hugged and kissed, and the children gathered round. "Where have you been, father?" a daughter asked.

"You've been gone a year," another daughter said.

"A year?" Taylor repeated. "I've been gone a year?"

"Yes," Ann answered, gazing intently at her husband.

"Is it All Hallows' Eve?" Taylor asked.

"Yes," Ann replied.

"Is it 1822?"

"Yes. It is All Hallows' Eve, 1822," Ann said. "Why should you doubt this?"

"Where have you been, father?" the son asked.

"I've been away," Taylor said. "Please, let us eat something."

Ann fetched bread and ham and tea, and they ate and talked late into the night about the children and their activities the previous year. Early the next morning, while the children slept, Ann and her husband talked again.

"Betsy came back that night, the night you didn't come home," Ann said. "She went directly to the barn. We waited late into the night for your return. Betsy came home, and you didn't. We were terrified.

"For a year there was no evidence of your whereabouts, not a thing," Ann said. "We feared the worst. We thought maybe you'd died, or even been murdered by someone from one of your law cases. Rumors were rampant. There were awful stories. You know how people are.

"Where were you, husband?"

"I was far away."

"Where?"

"It's difficult to explain."

"Please try, husband."

"I was in the middle of the country."

"Kentucky?"

"No."

"Ohio?"

"Farther west," he said.

"Were you near the western border?" Ann asked. "I thought you said you were in the middle of the country."

"I was west of the Mississippi," Taylor said.

"Mississippi. The river?"

"Yes."

"That's Indian country," she declared.

"It is in the present day. In 1822."

"What?" Ann asked, looking puzzled. "What did you do there? For a year."

"I worked on a farm," he said. "We will talk about it, my love. Over time."

"Husband, have you had some sort of problem?"

"Yes. I've had a problem. However, I've seen things and learned of great events."

"Great events?"

"Yes," he said. "There will be great change and incredible things to come."

There was quiet, then Ann said, "You can talk about it in time, my love. I will not bother you until you are ready to speak of it."

"Thank you, my love," Taylor said. "You have a noble spirit."

As the years passed, Taylor thought often of his time in the modern world. Sometimes, at his law office, he got out the duffel bag and examined the clothes from the year he spent in the modern world. He would put on the baseball cap and have a look in the mirror. He thought of Carl and Doris and things like refrigeration and electric lights. And he always remembered the abundance, the unbelievable plenty of the modern world, and how modern people didn't seem to appreciate what they had. Maybe his grandchildren would share in that bounty in the earlier years of the new world of plenty.

Of course, Taylor understood that, despite the abundance of the modern world, things hadn't really changed. There was still misery and cruelty and war. And he wondered if the prosperity would last.

One day, Taylor got out the bills and coins that he'd kept from the modern world. He studied the nickel, the one with Mr. Jefferson on it, then looked at a dollar bill with General

Washington's image. Then he ran his fingers across the five-dollar note with Abraham Lincoln, the president who fought to save the Union and freed the slaves.

Like others of his time, Taylor watched the growth of regional conflict in the country. Unlike others, Taylor knew the result of that escalating clash. He knew of the Civil War to come and its awful death and destruction. And he could do nothing about it. So he worked, tended to his five acres, and, most of all, loved his wife and children. And he did write a will for MacFall, the tavern owner, and his wife.

Over the years, Taylor often told Ann about his time in the modern world. He told her numerous times in great detail about the Halloween night when his ride in the dark woods was interrupted by the appearance of a four-lane highway, a road from the modern world. He told Ann about the Larkins and their home on wheels and of the great building in the city of millions that reached to the sky. And he spoke of historical events and great inventions to come.

Ann listened to his stories, but she usually didn't say much. Mostly, she just listened. However, after Taylor showed her his clothes and the bills and coins from the modern world, her belief in his story grew. As the nation's descent into greater conflict supported her husband's unwavering prediction of civil war, Ann seemed even more to believe her husband's story of the year he spent in the modern world, in a place with tidy towns amid endless waves of grain.

About the Author

Neal Lovett enjoys family, friends, and the outdoors.

About the Book

On Halloween night, 1821, Taylor's ride through the woods is interrupted, and he is taken to another place.

Printed and bound by PG in the USA